T IS WALKER BOOK BELONGS TO:

_____

_____

_____

Colin McNaughton

When I Grow Up

WALKER BOOKS

AND SUBSIDIARIES

LONDON · BOSTON · SYDNEY · AUCKLAND

"Ladies and Gentlemen, welcome along to a musical packed with action and song. Sit back in your seats, we are ready to go – so strike up the band and it's on with the show!"

"When I grow up
I'd like to be
An explorer
Of the galaxy."

"**W**hen I grow up
I'd like to be
King of the jungle –

Wheee

Be careful, Colin!

"When I grow up,
Well, I just know it,
I will become
A famous poet."

"When I grow up
I'd like to be
An angel
Oh so heavenly."

"When I grow up,
Well, bless my soul,
I'll be the king
Of rock 'n' roll!"

"When we grow up

We'd like to be

The best
boy band

In
history."

"**W**hen I grow up
I'd like to be
Married with
A family."

"When we grow up, Miss,
Me and Joan,
We'd like a sweet shop
Of our own."

"When I grow up
I'd like to be

Rich and famous
On TV."

"**W**hen I grow up
I'd like to be

Called
'Your Royal Majesty'."

"When I grow up
I'd like to be
A mermaid in
The deep blue sea."

g–g–grow   up

I'd

l–like

t–t–to

b–b–be

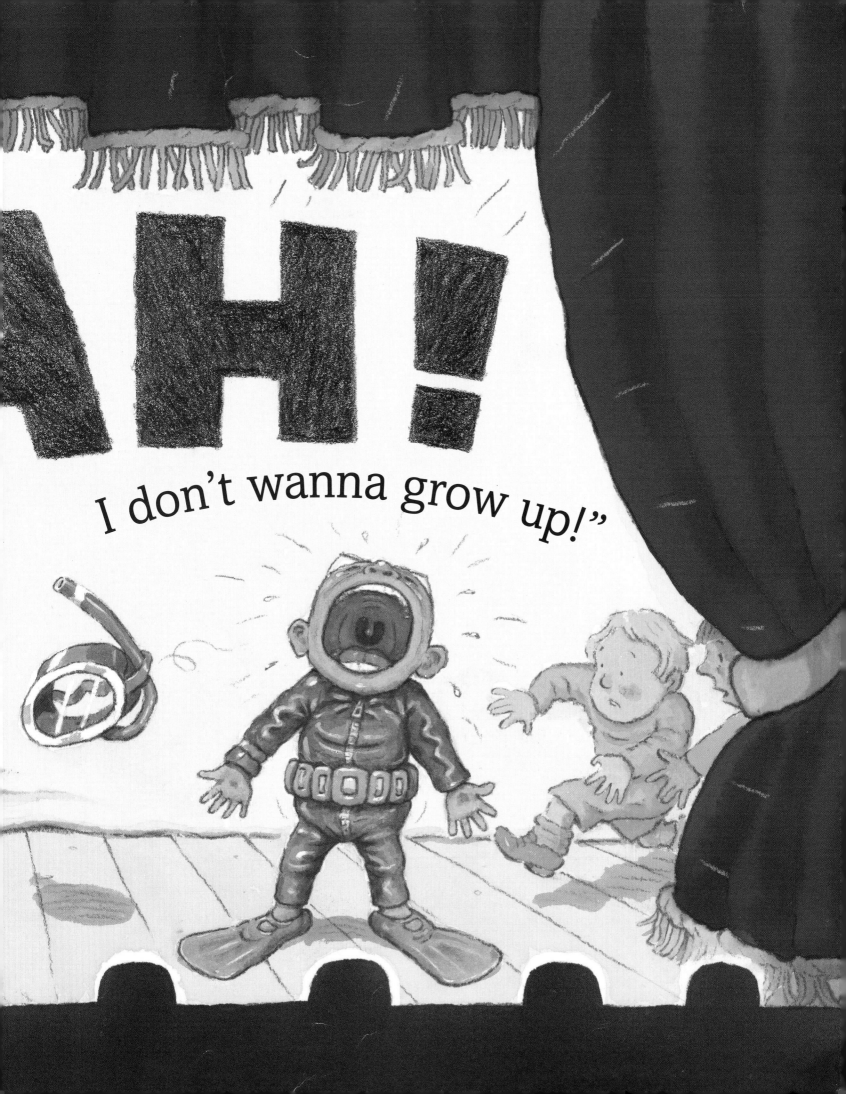

"There, there, sweetheart,
don't you fret,
You don't have to
grow up *yet*.
(I know *lots* of
grown-ups who
Still don't know
what they want to do.)

Enjoy your childhood
while you may –
Growing up is
years away!"